ABOUT THE ALDEN ALL STARS

Nothing's more important to Nick, Sam, Justin, and Dennis than their team, the Alden Panthers. Whether the sport is football, basketball, baseball, or soccer, the four seventh-graders can always be found practicing, sweating, and giving their all. Sometimes the Panthers are on their way to a winning season, and sometimes the team can't do anything right. But no matter what, you can be sure the ALDEN ALL STARS are playing to win.

Chock-full of plays, sports details, and plenty of exciting sports action, the ALDEN ALL STARS series is just right for anyone who loves to compete—or just loves a good story.

Shot from Midfield

ALDEN ALL STARS

Shot from Midfield

Tommy Hallowell

PUFFIN BOOKS

PUFFIN BOOKS
Published by the Penguin Group
Viking Penguin, a division of Penguin Books USA Inc.,
375 Hudson Street, New York, New York 10014, U.S.A.
Penguin Books Ltd, 27 Wrights Lane, London W8 5TZ, England
Penguin Books Australia Ltd, Ringwood, Victoria, Australia
Penguin Books Canada Ltd, 10 Alcorn Avenue, Toronto, Ontario, Canada M4V 3B2
Penguin Books (N.Z.) Ltd, 182–190 Wairau Road, Auckland 10, New Zealand

Penguin Books Ltd, Registered Offices: Harmondsworth, Middlesex, England

First published in Puffin Books, 1990
3   5   7   9   10   8   6   4   2
Copyright © Daniel Weiss and Associates, 1990
All rights reserved

LIBRARY OF CONGRESS CATALOGING IN PUBLICATION DATA
Hallowell, Tommy.   Shot from midfield / Tommy Hallowell.
p.   cm.–(Alden All Stars)
Summary: Justin finally gets to prove his athletic abilities when
he goes to summer soccer camp for three weeks.
ISBN 0-14-032912-9
[1. Soccer–Fiction.   2. Camps–Fiction.]   I. Title.   II. Series:
Hallowell, Tommy.   Alden All Stars.
PZ7.H164Sh 1990   [Fic]–dc20   89-78151

Printed in the United States of America
Set in Century Schoolbook

For the taller of the Hill brothers.

Shot from Midfield

1

Looking back over his shoulder as he ran, Justin Johnson watched the goalie drop the ball onto his foot and send a booming punt high into the summer sky. The ball hung in the air as Justin tried to guess where it would come down.

After a quick glance around at his teammates— the shirts in this pickup game of shirts-and-skins— he decided he should make a challenge for it. One of the skins' forwards had settled under the ball. Justin had time to get there, but he hung back a little, hoping that the guy wouldn't be able to control the ball.

Sure enough, the forward failed to trap the ball with his chest. It bounced off him and out of his reach. Already running, Justin swept up the ball and took off.

He cleared the midfield line and ten yards more before a defender approached. Justin slowed, hemmed in by the sideline. Looking for support he caught sight of Nick Wilkerson close behind. In one swift movement, Justin faked a dribble down the sideline to draw his man over, then fed a pass to Nick. Once the pass was off, Justin broke past the defender. Nick saw the move and fed him the ball again, a perfect wall pass.

Now Justin had room to move again, and he headed in, toward the middle of the field. Only one player stood between him and the goalie. He stopped the ball, and then, at the last possible moment, flicked it forward through the sweeper's legs, and sprinted after it.

The goalkeeper, watching the play, had ranged far off his line to cut down the angle. The two approached the ball but Justin got there first. With the goalie bearing down on him, he didn't have much room to shoot on either side, so he chipped directly under the ball, lifting a soft lob just over the goalie's outstretched hands. The ball floated lazily in the air, but there was no stopping it. It bounced once, twice, then crossed the goal line. The game's first goal!

Justin took his teammates' congratulations with a quiet smile, but he felt wildly happy. He had been worried about how good everyone was. Back in Cranbrook, where hardly anyone played soccer, he was the star. It was his best sport. But now he was at soccer camp, and he didn't know how he would stack up against 150 guys who liked soccer enough to come spend three whole weeks doing nothing but playing.

All his doubts disappeared with the goal. Justin knew he was going to like it here.

After the game broke up, Nick and Justin headed back to Bunk Michigan, where they had put all their stuff when they arrived that morning. Then they took a look around the camp.

"I wish we were in Bunk Florida," said Nick.

"Why?" said Justin.

"I'd like to be near the ocean."

But Justin wanted to talk about the game they'd just played. "So what do you think?" he asked. "The guys in that game weren't any better than us, right?"

"Maybe."

"C'mon, you think we're out of our league?"

"Maybe you aren't, but I haven't been playing soccer every spare minute of my life. I'm not so sure about me."

"Forget it, Nick, you'll do fine."

"I felt kinda lost out there this morning, you know? I dribbled and shot as well as the others, but I didn't know what strategy to use, or how to set up plays or anything."

"I supppose that's what we came here to learn."

"We? What are *you* going to learn?"

"Nothing, I already know it all," Justin said with a laugh.

"I don't know how I let you talk me into coming to soccer camp."

"Get out of here," said Justin. "I didn't twist your arm. You could have stayed with Dennis and Sam and played Algonquin League."

"I know, I know. I'm just on your case. This place looks great," said Nick. "I'll have fun even if I stink up the joint."

Their other two best friends, Dennis and Sam, had decided to stay in Cranbrook and play for the local baseball league. The four of them didn't split up often. All last year, their first year at Alden Junior High, they had hung out together, and had played on the football, basketball, and baseball teams.

4

It was true that Justin had played more soccer than Nick. Justin's father had played for his college soccer team, and the two of them would often go out in the yard and kick the ball around until dinnertime. Justin played other sports, but soccer was his true love. Unfortunately, there wasn't a soccer team at Alden. It didn't start until ninth grade. Justin could hardly wait.

In other sports, being a good team player was enough for him. Making a contribution. Solid. Dependable. But now Justin wanted more. This was his one chance to shine. This was soccer. *His* sport.

2

"Go," the counselor said, clicking his stopwatch.

Justin tapped the ball forward to the left of the first cone, then with the outside of his foot to get around it. With the stopwatch running, he was to dribble through the slalom course and back as fast as possible. Watching the players before him, he thought they had wasted too much time in hitting the ball back and forth from leg to leg. By pushing it forward accurately, Justin minimized the number of times he had to touch the ball.

He ran comfortably. It was just like the little dribbling course he had set up in his own backyard with his father. He paced himself. Some of the others had lost control trying to go too fast. He turned at the last cone and headed back, quick, but totally in control. The counselor hit the stopwatch as Justin finished.

"Great time," he said, writing it down on his clipboard, then reading the name. "Justin Johnson. Did you ever play on a team, Justin?"

"No, not really."

The counselor just nodded.

As his group moved together through all the stations, Justin's confidence grew. The other guys were impressed. His time in the hundred-yard dash was average—Nick did the best—but in almost every other event, Justin excelled. At the juggling stop each player was given a ball and was supposed to keep it in the air for as long as possible, using knees, head, chest, and feet. Justin had been practicing juggling alone for so many years, he was unstoppable. One by one, the others lost control after a minute, a minute and a half, but Justin kept going. After two minutes and ten seconds he was the only one left. After five minutes, the counselor told him he could stop.

"Where'd you learn to do that?" asked one kid.

"I don't know. I guess from my dad."

"That's awesome."

Justin shrugged coolly, but he liked what he was hearing.

All afternoon, Justin was impressive. The only stop where he had trouble was serving balls over 40 yards. His first try was only 25 yards in the air. He had never thought he was a weak kicker, but all the other guys were easily clearing 40, 45 yards. He had two more tries, but his long was just 35.

As they moved to the next stop, Justin was shaking his head in disappointment.

"What are you down about?" Nick asked. "So what if you don't have a power kick? You've dominated every other test."

"I guess you're right," said Justin. "But I'm just surprised. I always thought I could drive the ball pretty well."

"Maybe you just got nervous after you mis-hit that first one. Maybe you tried too hard."

The next event was heading at goal and Justin made eight out of his ten chances, two better than anyone else. His good mood returned. All in all, Justin felt confident when they finished up the last event. He had made an impression. Of course, he hadn't seen the players in the other groups yet, but the counselors seemed to think he was very good.

At dinner, the head counselors gave introductory speeches. Tomorrow morning the teams would be announced and everyone would change bunks to be with their team.

"If you have special requests for bunkmates," said a tall counselor, "we'll write them down after dinner, and take them into consideration—but we can't guarantee anything." Justin and Nick looked at each other, realizing that they might not be placed in the same bunk.

After dinner, the two friends waited in the large group of kids making such requests. Then there was a free period. There was a softball game, a basketball game, and some other stuff going on. But most of the campers just hung out throwing Frisbees or sat talking. Nick and Justin wandered around for a little while. They watched the basketball game.

"Want to try to get in?" asked Nick.

"I don't know," said Justin. "Want to get a soccer ball and kick it around?"

"Geez, we've been playing soccer all day."

"Yeah, well, we don't have to."

"No, you're right. We're here to play soccer."

They got a ball and went out to one of the soccer

fields. Another kid came by and watched them for a minute.

Justin caught his eye and pointed to the ball. The kid jogged in a little, nodding, so Justin passed him the ball. He trapped it and kicked it back to Nick.

"My name's Nick, and this is Justin," said Nick.

"I'm Tony, Tony Fripp. Hi."

"You been here before?" asked Justin, as they continued to practice passing.

"No, first year. You?"

"Same. Both of us."

Another guy joined them and they made up a little two-on-two dribbling game and played until they heard the three whistles that signaled the end of the activity period.

They split up to go to their bunks and Nick and Justin took the ball back to the equipment bin. The sun was just setting as they made their way back to Bunk Michigan.

It was weird, being with guys you didn't know, and tomorrow they would be with a different group. Nick and Justin listened to a couple of campers who had been there last year, Brian and Wally.

"You think dinner was okay, but just wait till you try to eat the pancakes," Brian said.

"Yeah, the elephant scabs," Wally agreed.

"Gross!" another kid said.

"It's great," Brian went on. "You can press the pancakes down and then pass the tray all around the table upside down and they stick."

Justin and Nick exchanged glances. They both thought Brian was funny, but he was obviously showing off, making a big deal about knowing all the ins and outs from last year.

"So what happens tomorrow, with the teams?" asked another newcomer.

"They announce the teams first thing after breakfast," Brian said. "Then everyone moves their stuff and they issue everyone the balls."

"Everyone gets soccer balls?" Nick asked.

"Yeah," said Wally. "Every camper gets a ball and you write your name on it right away."

"And if you lose it, it's gone," Brian said.

"And when they announce the teams they announce captains, too. It's usually the best players."

"I was a captain last year," Brian boasted. Again, Justin and Nick glanced at each other.

After a while, the counselor told them all to change for bed, and then turned out the lights. The dark didn't stop them from talking, though.

"So do we start playing games right away?" Nick asked.

"Pretty much," Wally said. "There's a regular league, with standings and everything."

"Each bunk plays the other nine bunks one game each, and then at the end of the year there's a big tournament for the camp championship."

"What do you get if you win?" one guy asked.

"You get to go home," Nick joked. The others laughed.

"You get nothing," Wally said. "You just get to win."

"What if you have the best record in the season, but lose in the tournament?" Justin asked.

"Same difference," Brian said.

"No trophies? Arm patches? Certificates? C'mon, you must get something."

"Everyone gets stuff like that on awards day, the last day of camp," Brian said. "But it's dumb, you know? They don't have an all-star team, they just give out awards like 'best hustle' and 'most improved' on each team."

"All right, boys," said the counselor. "That's enough chatter. Let's simmer down and go to sleep."

Brian started to say something else, but the counselor interrupted him.

"What I mean is—no more talking. Got it?"

Even in the silence, Justin found it hard to sleep.

His mind was racing. He was still full of questions about the season, the daily schedule, practices, activities. Would he and Nick be on the same team? And more than anything else, Justin wondered if he would be good—a star—or just another player.

3

So far, four bunks had been read and neither Nick nor Justin had been called. Joe Malone, the head counselor, stood reading from his clipboard in the center of the quad. Justin was getting antsy.

"Okay, that's all for Bunk Oklahoma," Joe called out. "Please keep the noise down! All right. Bunk Vermont: Captain, Justin Johnson."

Justin couldn't believe it. Captain! They thought he was really good! He was so excited he almost

14

forgot to listen for Nick's name, but when he turned to smile at his friend, he remembered.

"Hey, *Captain*," Nick said, under his breath.

"Sshh!" Justin hushed him, listening intently.

"Michael Bender, Kirk Flaherty, Dana Edwards, Tony Fripp . . ."

"We met him," Nick said, trying to act as though he wasn't worried about possibly being in a different bunk. Justin waved him quiet again.

"Steve Kincaid, Cosimo Vitorelli, Nick Wilkerson . . ."

"Yesss!" Justin said and the two friends slapped hands happily.

"Lou Smith, Marty Johannson, Woody Widmer, Phil Thompson," Joe continued. "Okay, your counselors are Ian Roper and Pete Frumkin. That's Bunk Vermont. Quiet down! Nobody leaves till we've read every bunk."

After more whistles, threats, and shouting, he managed to finish the last list and dismiss the group. Everyone scrambled to their feet and rushed to their new bunks.

"Couldn't be better," Justin said. "We're together and we don't have that Brian Packer guy or his pal Wally on our team."

"But it's terrible." Nick frowned.

"What's the matter? We're in the same bunk."

"Bunk Vermont. *Vermont.* What a crummy name," Nick said, and Justin smiled. "Not only that, but we've got a kid named Cosmo."

"Co*si*mo," corrected a short stocky kid right behind them.

Nick smiled sheepishly.

"Just kidding, sorry. I'm Nick," he said, nodding. The kid eyed him suspiciously for a moment, then smiled.

"Cosmo," he said, trying out the sound of it. "I could live with that."

Once they had all gathered in Bunk Vermont there was another round of introductions. Their counselor was a short, muscular guy who was wearing an Ohio State T-shirt.

"Listen up, everyone, let's not all talk at once. Let me introduce myself. I'm Pete Frumkin. My friends call me Frumkin, so you might as well, too."

He had everyone say where they were from and what position they liked to play. Almost all were first-year campers. Only Dana Edwards, a tall red-headed kid, and a quiet kid named Steve Kincaid had been there before. The other counselor, Ian Roper, was from England.

"All right, then," said Frumkin, glancing at his

watch. "Now we all know each other. In twenty minutes, we all go for a workout. Oh, that reminds me."

He went to the back of the bunk and opened a
closet. Out came an avalanche of soccer balls. The
nearest boys grabbed them as they rolled into the
room.

"These are your soccer balls. This is an indelible
marker. No one leaves the bunk until their name is
on a ball." He passed the pen to Steve Kincaid, while
the other campers each grabbed a ball.

"After lunch," Frumkin continued, "we come back
here for an hour rest period and at two o'clock Bunk
Vermont plays its first game."

"A game?" Cosimo exclaimed.

"Today?" Woody Widmer chipped in.

"What's the matter, aren't you ready to go?" Ian
said with a laugh.

"Shouldn't we practice or something first?" Justin
asked.

"Look, guys," Frumkin said. "It's just a game. You
all know how to play and we want to see how you
do in a game situation. And anyway, you'll be getting
plenty of drills and practice around here. Believe me,
in a week you'll be begging for a game instead of
more coaching."

"What positions will we play?" Steve asked.

"You'll play wherever we tell you to, all right?" Ian said. "Now everybody out of the bunk. We'll see you at lunch."

As they started to leave, Frumkin said: "Oh, by the way, start thinking of a team nickname. We'll vote and choose one at rest hour."

Tony joined Nick and Justin as they wandered up to the basketball court. The three of them shot baskets and chatted.

"You're pretty good, Tony," Nick said, watching him make a fourth straight outside shot. "Play for your school team?"

"Nah," Tony said as he dribbled. "I'm way too short."

He was right. Justin himself was not tall, but stood half-a-head taller than Tony.

"I was on the wrestling team during the winter anyway. How 'bout you guys? Did you play basketball?" Tony asked.

"Not me," Justin said, "but Nick was the starting point guard, and the team won the league championship, too."

The three played until lunch. At rest hour, Bunk Vermont discussed names for their team.

"All right, as captain, Justin, you'll have to run the voting," Frumkin said.

"Okay, uh, any suggestions?" Luckily, Justin had Nick to help him out.

"Vampires, Vermont Vampires," Nick said.

"That's good," said Cosimo.

"No, let's get a normal name, a soccer name like Rowdies or Cosmos," Dana suggested.

"How about the Cosimos?" Cosimo laughed.

"No way!" a chorus of voices shouted.

"We need a V-word, vermin, violins, vultures—how about vultures?" Steve suggested.

"The Vermont Vultures: We eat dead meat!" Nick said.

"Should we vote?" Justin asked.

"You're the captain," Dana said.

"Okay, okay. Any votes for, what'd you say, Vampires?"

After all the names had been voted on, they chose the Vermont Vultures.

As scheduled, the Vultures took to the field at two o'clock. Ian rallied them together.

"Here's the lineup," Ian began.

"Does this game count in the standings?" Justin interrupted.

"Yes," Ian answered, and a mumble of discontent went around. "Now, listen up, we'll play a four-three-three. Four fullbacks—one a sweeper and one a stopper—three midfielders and three strikers. By the way, don't be surprised to find Frumkin or me out on the field. For these early games, we'll roam around a bit."

He read out the positions. Justin was placed at center midfield. He knew it was a key position. As the main linkman, he would quarterback the team. Nick was at sweeper. Justin knew that would change. Nick was a speedy goal-scorer, a perfect wing or striker. Defense wasn't his spot. Marty Johannson was the Vultures' goalkeeper.

"Ready or not, here we go," Tony chuckled as he and Justin took the field. Tony was at center striker.

The other team, Bunk Ohio, kicked off and took the ball deep into Vulture territory, but Dana Edwards tackled the ball away from a forward and then sent a booming clearing pass all the way over midfield. Justin corralled the ball. He had played games in gym class before, but this was different. It was a real game in a real league, and every player was good.

Justin fed the ball to Cosimo, who was free, but the next pass went awry and Ohio took over.

Throughout the first half, Justin played well. With both teams so unorganized, there were many scoring opportunities. Vermont led 3–2 at the half. Justin had assisted on two of the goals. Cosimo had scored two and Kirk Flaherty had scored the other.

The positions were shifted around for the second half, but Justin stayed at center half. Early on, he made a great lead pass to Kirk, who took it right at the goal. The shot was saved but deflected back into play. Lou Smith hammered it in for the score.

"Maestro!" Ian yelled happily from the sidelines.

"What?" Justin said, running toward his coach.

"That was a lovely push. Lovely!"

"Push?"

"Push, yes, I guess you Americans call it a pass."

Later, Justin brought up the ball again, but he kept waiting for an opening, dribbling back and forth until finally he was trapped by a second marking player and lost the ball. Ian was by him again.

"You're thinking too much, Justin," Ian said, jogging along with him downfield. "Not every pass has to break them wide open. Just pass and move, pass and move."

Justin nodded, but he wasn't so sure. It seemed like nit-picking criticism. Since he wasn't big or strong, or even particularly fast, Justin felt like "thinking" was his main weapon. He wanted to show Ian that he could analyze and play well at the same time.

Kirk scored again to finish off the Vermont Vultures' first victory, 5–3. Ian talked about the game afterward. The main thing he stressed was staying spread out more, not crashing in on the ball. They were all tired, but Ian ran heading and dribbling drills, before letting the team go for a swim.

After they changed, Nick, Dana, and Justin walked down to the waterfront.

"You guys both played great today," Dana said.

"You, too," said Nick.

"I didn't play so great," Justin disagreed.

"Sure, you did," Dana insisted.

"Yeah? What'd I do that was so great?"

"Well, you know, passing and that assist," Dana answered.

"Two assists," Nick corrected.

"Did I score?" Justin asked.

"Well . . ." Dana began.

"No, I didn't. I played okay, but that's not 'great' by a long shot."

4

"I can hardly believe this is only our second full day," Justin said at his bunk's lunch table in the cafeteria.

"Yeah, isn't it incredible?" Tony said.

"I know what you mean," Kirk put in. "I feel like I've known all you guys forever."

"Do you like seafood?" Woody Widmer asked Kirk between bites of his peanut butter and banana sandwich.

"Sure," Kirk responded, and Woody opened his

mouth wide, right in Kirk's face.

"See? Food!" Woody said with a laugh.

"You're seriously weird, Woody," said Kirk.

"You guys will be amazed at how fast camp is over, too," Dana said.

"Was your team good last year?" Nick asked.

"At first we were rotten, but we got better. Got creamed in the tournament, though."

"What happens if you lose in the first round? That's it, no more games?" Steve asked.

"Nah, you play the consolation games, whoop-de-doo," Dana said.

"Do you think we're good?" Steve asked Dana.

"Are you kidding?" Nick interrupted. "Vultures rule! No consolation games for us, we go to the championship or die trying."

"We've got a serious chance," Dana said. "But it's too early to tell. There are some pretty good players here."

"Who's the best player in camp?" Cosimo asked.

"Justin," Nick answered quickly.

"You know who's really good?" Dana said. "Brian Packer. He plays attack, he's a great shooter, and he led the league last year when he was only eleven. Now he's twelve."

"That dweeb?" Nick scoffed.

"I don't like him, either," Dana said. "But he's good."

"Justin would kill him at juggling, dribbling, passing. Wouldn't you, Justin?"

"I don't know." Justin shrugged.

"You're definitely our best passer," Cosimo said.

Big compliment, Justin thought.

"That kid who played defense for Ohio was pretty good, too," Steve said. "He was all over the field. Hey, Frumkin, who's the best?"

"Yeah, you know everybody," Nick said. "It's Justin, right?"

"You're all good players," Frumkin said. All the Vultures booed him.

"Chicken!" Dana called him. "C'mon, at least do you think we can win the championship?"

"Yes, I do," Frumkin said. "And so can Michigan and Montana and Wisconsin and . . ."

Again, he was met with a chorus of booing.

After rest hour, they did drills. Two-on-one drills, dribbling drills, and other basic exercises. Justin's favorite was something called center circle kick-out. Every player started in the center circle, trying to keep control of his own ball, while kicking out the other players' balls to eliminate them. The last one in the circle won. Three times, Justin got to be one of the last two. Against Nick, Kirk, and Cosimo. He beat Nick, but lost to Kirk and Cosimo.

This afternoon they played their second game, against Bunk Montana.

Now they were starting to work together as a team. Frumkin and Ian had coached them so they knew where they were supposed to be going, and when.

Montana scored first, on a corner kick that was headed just past Marty's outstretched arms. Justin was there to help him up.

"Nothing you could do, Marty," Justin said, pulling him to his feet.

"I should have gone to the ball before the header."

"No," said Dana. "I'm the one who should have stopped that guy. I timed my jump all wrong."

"Let's go get it back," Justin said, clapping Dana's hand. "Let's go, Vultures."

The game continued. Justin trailed the play as Kirk brought the ball up the right side. Kirk accelerated, trying to get around his man, but without success. He pulled up again and fed it back to Justin, who immediately passed to Cosimo on his left. Cosimo was very quick. He scooted inside, past a fullback. As the defense converged on Cosimo, Justin found himself open as he circled in behind. But Cosimo couldn't see him, and tried a difficult cross to Tony. Tony and a Montana player got to it at the same time, with Tony throwing a rock-hard sliding tackle. The ball banged past the Montana fullback and over everybody, except Justin. Justin controlled the ball with no one between him and the goal. It was an easy chance, but there was no time to waste. He took one step with the ball and shot as hard as he could, aiming for the near post.

Watching his shot, he held his breath, trying to coax it past the keeper. *C'mon, c'mon. Get in!*

But the ball was floating too much. The keeper dove and deflected it out and over the goal line. Justin couldn't believe he had blown such an easy chance.

"C'mon, Justin! Organize your corner kick!" Frumkin yelled from the sideline.

Justin looked up. He had been thinking so much about the shot, he had forgotten that it was his job to call the play on the corner. Kirk was waiting for him.

"Far side," Justin said, then ran back to tell key

players. Kirk's cross was short, and easily inter-
cepted by Montana's defense, who cleared.

Near the end of the first half, Dana Edwards
single-handedly tied up the game. He made an end-
to-end run, finishing off the play with a driving
twenty-yard shot that found the top right corner of
the net.

He was surrounded by happy teammates.

"Sweeper run wild!" Nick exclaimed.

"What a run!" Tony chirped.

"Great goal." Justin joined in the congratulations,
but he couldn't help feeling jealous. Even defensemen were scoring now. If only he had some power
in his shot. Of course, it was easy for a big guy like
Dana to hit with power. It was just a matter of le-
verage.

In the second half, the Vultures really took control
of the game. Justin, Cosimo, and Kirk were all su-
perior ball handlers, so once they got it into the offensive end—and Dana got it to them plenty—they
could really work the ball around. They took the lead
when Justin stole the ball from the Montana defender and got off a quick feed to Cosimo, breaking
free right in front of the net. Moments later, he led
Woody Widmer with a wall pass that Woody put into

the upper right corner. He couldn't have thrown it with more perfect placement. So when the final whistle blew, Vermont had won their second game, by a 3–1 margin.

And Justin had two more assists.

5

"Did you hear about Brian Packer?" Steve asked everyone at the dinner table that night.

"What do you mean?" Justin asked.

"Bunk Wisconsin beat Michigan thirteen to one."

"Thirteen!" Nick yelped.

"And Packer scored *ten*."

"Cripes, he wrapped up the summer's scoring title in one afternoon," Tony said, shaking his head.

"Michigan must be rotten," Nick said.

"Ten goals?" Justin asked again. "That's incredible. It's like every five minutes, boom, another goal."

"Scoring goals is easy if all the other parts of your game, and your team, are working," Ian reminded his campers.

"Yeah, yeah, teamwork, passing, defense, we know," Tony said.

"Well, what we ought to do is have a peek at this Brian lad playing and see how we'd defend against him, right?"

"When do we play Wisconsin?" Kirk asked.

"Day after tomorrow," Justin answered. He had already checked the schedule. "Hey, let's see if they'll scrimmage us tonight, after dinner."

"Yeah, let's do it," Nick agreed.

"I already signed up for a hobby hour," Cosimo said.

Nick held a clenched fist in his face. "I'll give you your hobby hour right in the face."

"All right, all right."

"Can we go ask their table?" Tony asked Frumkin.

"Sure. Justin, you go."

Justin walked across the dining room, scanning the Wisconsin table until he recognized Brian Packer.

"Uh, hi, Brian. You guys want to play a scrimmage game after dinner?"

"What bunk?" Brian said.

"Vermont."

"What are you, the captain?"

"Yeah."

"I remember you. You're a real good juggler."

"Thanks."

"So maybe you'll get a job in the circus." The table roared with laughter. Justin blushed.

"Do you want to play or don't you?" Justin asked again.

"Bunk challenge, huh?"

"Just for practice."

"Just for practice—we'll kick yer butts. What do we say, Wisconsin? Up for a little Vermont pounding after dinner?"

They all sounded agreement.

"Deal," Brian said, and abruptly turned away. Justin just rolled his eyes and walked back.

"We're on," he told his teammates.

The two teams met on the near field twenty minutes after dinner. They agreed to play for forty-five minutes or until they got called in to the bunks.

It didn't take long for Justin to see that Brian was for real. Brian took a pass and made a run through the Vermont defense that made them look like they all had two left feet. Not only that, but when they finally did force him wide-right, he didn't take a desperate shot, as Justin expected. Instead Brian controlled the ball and brought it back out.

Ten minutes into the game, Brian took a long cross and half-volleyed a rocketing shot into the upper right-hand corner of the goal. Marty dived after it, but never had a chance.

A few minutes later, Justin fed Nick ahead on the left sideline. Nick tried to run past his man, but couldn't turn the corner on him, so he brought the ball back out and passed it back to Justin. Looking for an open man, Justin suddenly noticed that a second defender was coming at him. He quickly turned the ball away, looking for a quick outlet pass, but before he got it off, he was hit with a sliding tackle. He felt like someone had run into him with a bicycle.

His legs cut out from under him, Justin collapsed in a heap as the ball squirted away, where it was picked up by a Wisconsin player.

"Foul!" Justin yelled, still on the ground. He glanced at his attacker. It was Brian.

"Foul? No way. You're crazy," Brian barked.

"You mugged me!"

"I got the ball," Brian said, pointing ahead to it.

"And my shin and my ankle and my chest. C'mon, Brian, that was a foul."

"No way."

At that, Brian simply jogged downfield, where play had continued. Justin shook his head. Maybe they shouldn't have played without a counselor or referee.

The game grew rougher. Wally and Cosimo both got taken down by Wisconsin body checks. Then Dana creamed a Wisconsin player as they both went up for a header. Still, the usual rules didn't apply, forcing the Vultures to adjust. Justin made sure that he, and his teammates, never held the ball for long. Quick passes and constant movement was the key.

Soon their movement off the ball started to work. Cosimo took a pass and on one-touch got it to Justin. He held it for a moment, and Brian attacked, committing himself too far in. Justin went right back to Cosimo and flew by Brian for the return pass. Veering toward goal, Justin drew the sweeper's attention. Then, at the last possible moment he sent a hopeful crossing pass to the other side of the field, where Nick and Steve had a two-on-one advantage. Nick controlled the ball and shot a low liner into the near side for the tying goal.

Celebrating, Justin ran toward Nick, but suddenly he was falling. Someone had tripped him. He thumped to the ground, catching himself, and turned to see Brian backing away. *What a complete diphead,* Justin thought. *I'm not going to forget this.*

Over the next few minutes, Vermont gave Wisconsin a taste of their own medicine. With all the body-checking going on it looked like a hockey game. Tempers were really starting to flare. It was probably a good thing that the final argument was over an offsides penalty. Wisconsin called offside on Cosimo—Justin could see that he was onside, close, but onside—and stopped playing. Cosimo went in toward goal, and shot, but the goalie didn't even try to save it. He just stood there pointing to where they were calling the offsides.

Cosimo was steaming.

"What are you talking about! This guy was right with me."

Three or four players from each side were yelling all at once.

"You were off."

"He was not. I could see him. . . ."

"No goal . . ."

"What!"

"Anyway, we didn't even try after the offsides."

"We should get a penalty shot, from the spot he shot."

"Forget it. He was off."

"No way."

"We're not taking this crap."

"You gotta play by the rules," Justin yelled.

"We don't gotta play nothin'," Brian yelled right back. "We're out of here."

"Go ahead," Woody yelled after them as the Wisconsin players walked away. "We'll just see who wins when we have a referee."

"We win, I guess," Cosimo said.

"Sort of," Justin shrugged.

"Wouldn't you like to see Brian get a flying wedgie?" Woody suggested, as they headed to the bunk.

"Yeah," Cosimo agreed. "And given by Hulk Hogan."

6

After breakfast Wednesday there was a free activity period. Nick wanted to go fishing, so Justin went along. They borrowed fishing equipment and life preservers down by the boathouse, and took a rowboat out onto the lake. Soon they were floating lazily in a cove away from the swiming area, watching their bobbers and basking in the sunshine.

Justin sighed. "I was just thinking about that shot I messed up yesterday."

"Shot you messed up? Against Wisconsin?"

"No, the regular game, Montana. You know, the easy chance that I just lofted right into the goalie's hands."

"You didn't mess up. You had a good shot and you took it. He made a good save, a diving save," Nick insisted.

"Nah, it was a weak effort. I just don't have any power. Zilch."

"You've got plenty. Anyway, we came to this camp to learn, so maybe Frumkin or Ian can show you how to get more power."

"I doubt it. I know how to kick. I know how to play this game. I'm just not strong enough."

They sat quietly for a while. Finally Nick spoke again.

"Well, power or not, you're the best player on the team, and you've led us to two wins already."

Justin shrugged and reeled in his line a bit. "But you're probably the only guy in the bunk who thinks I'm the best."

"No way."

"You heard them the other day. Half of them think Brian is the best player going, even if they hate him. And on our own team, you and Cosimo score more goals than I do."

"Me!" Nick yelped. "You're nuts. *Nobody* thinks I'm better than you."

"I just think that if I'm good I should score goals."

"Well, I guess everybody does."

"I want the other guys to . . . Hey, look at your bobber!"

Nick looked as the bobber plunged under the water.

"You've got something!"

"Woo-eee!" Nick yelped. He started reeling in furiously. The bobber was completely gone now. His line was taut. Justin leaned out. As the line got closer he could see the fish.

"Oh, man, it's a whale!" Nick howled.

He kept reeling and up came the fish.

"Some whale," Justin laughed. It was maybe eight inches long, a round silvery fish. "So what is it?"

"I don't know."

Nick held the rod up over the boat. The fish flapped in the air.

"Well, now what do we do?" Justin asked.

"I don't know," Nick said. "I've never gone fishing before. Have you?"

"No!" Justin laughed. "This was your big idea. I'm

not touching that slimy thing. For all we know, it has teeth."

Nick set his rod on the side of the boat, and pulled the line toward him.

"I guess I should take it off the hook and let it go," he said.

"We're sure not going to eat it for dinner."

"We could eat it right here, Justin. Sushi!"

Nick managed to get hold of the fish and work the hook out of its mouth, but as he did so, the fish slipped from his hand and into the boat. As he tried to grab the fish again, the boat rocked crazily.

"Hey, your rod!" Justin exclaimed. Nick's rod slid into the water. Justin grabbed the line, but the rod sank into the lake.

"Pull it in!"

"I'm trying," Justin said, pulling in the line hand over hand. "But it just keeps sinking."

Nick grabbed the fish and scooped it back into the lake. It zipped away into the dark water.

"Keep bringing in the line. It's gotta be attached to the rod."

By now the line was a tangled mess in the bottom of the rowboat.

"Okay, here it comes."

Now there was tension on the line and slowly, Justin pulled it up. Finally, the rod surfaced, covered with dark green plants and muck.

"Whew, at least we didn't lose it," Nick said with relief.

"Gross," Justin said, picking some of the stuff off it.

They spent the rest of the outing untangling the line, but they didn't mind. Anything was better than catching more fish.

Soon after they got back, Bunk Vermont got together for soccer practice. One of the drills they ran was give-and-go shooting. While Marty and Phil took turns manning the goal, each player passed it to Ian, who fed them a return pass that they would shoot.

Justin was determined to test his strength again. Maybe Nick was right and he did shoot hard enough. Maybe he had just been unlucky on his shots. His turn arrived. He pushed the ball to Ian and when the return came, wound up and walloped the ball. It was a hard shot, but well to the right, missing the goal.

"You don't have to boot the stuffing out of it, Justin. Placement, placement, placement!" Ian yelled.

Justin retrieved his ball and returned to the back of the line. Nick had gone just before him.

"That was a pretty hard kick," Nick said.

"Yeah, and five yards off," Justin scoffed.

They took a couple more turns. Each time Justin tried to kill the ball he mis-hit. As Nick was about to go again, he stopped to ask a question.

"Ian, how do I get more power on my shot?"

Justin knew exactly what Nick was doing: asking the question he, Justin, should have asked.

"First off, you're all trying too hard. You're falling over backward. Shooting is ninety percent timing and aim. Pure power isn't necessary."

"But it helps," Tony said.

"It can help," Ian agreed. "But you're all throwing yourselves back—when I keep telling you to keep your weight forward."

"It's like a baseball swing," Frumkin added. "You guys are all 'pulling the ball' trying to jerk a home run, but you've got to move your weight forward, and only in the follow-through does your weight go back."

"Don't know baseball," Ian said, "but there's another thing. Come here, Nick. Show me your instep drive in slow motion."

"My what?"

"Your shot, a regular shot."

Nick performed in slow motion.

"There, stop," Ian said, and Nick froze. "What did we say in the basic instruction on shooting?"

No one remembered.

"Look at his knee—fully extended and he hasn't even touched the ball yet," Ian said excitedly. "Your knee stays bent for power and low trajectory. Then, when you're *driving* through the ball, the knee is still adding momentum. Otherwise you might as well be swinging a cricket bat at it. A baseball bat, whatever. All right, let's see it."

Nick took his turn, but he was thinking so much about all the advice he mis-hit the ball. Then Justin's turn came. He hit the ball with a carefully bent knee, but the shot just lofted up into the air, where Marty caught it easily.

"Good," Ian said.

"Good? That was terrible . . ." Justin began to protest.

"Forget the shot, your leg was right on. It was soft because you got under it."

Lunchtime was nearing, so they only ran through the drill one more time. Justin shot with a bent knee, but this time tried hard to stay on top of the ball and drive it. He stubbed his toe hard into the ground and the ball squirted harmlessly to the right of the goal.

Another practice was over. Justin's toe hurt.

7

The Vultures lost to Bunk Nevada 2–0 that after-noon and afterward, Justin was in a bad mood. Most of the guys were hanging out in the bunk.

"I think I'll go shoot baskets," Nick said. "Want to come, Justin?"

"Go ahead," Justin answered. "I'm just going to vegetate."

A bunch of the guys headed out with Nick. Justin watched them leave. He wished he could have some of Nick's confidence. Whatever Nick did—like want-

ing to play basketball—the others would go along.
Everybody wanted to be Nick's best friend.

Justin, Kirk, Cosimo, and Marty stayed. Justin
was flipping through one of Ian's English soccer mag-
azines. Marty was playing a hand-held electronic
game and the blipping was the only sound in the
bunk until Cosimo struck up a conversation.

"Justin, do you think we should have beaten Nevada?"

"I don't know."

"You seem mad."

"I'm just tired."

"They were a good team. We didn't play badly, we
just didn't get the breaks."

"Guess so."

The conversation petered out. Justin didn't mind.
He just wanted to unwind. He couldn't complain
about not scoring goals. The guys would think he
was being selfish. Maybe he was, but it was frus-
trating. He knew he was good, so why couldn't he
finish a play? Twice today he had missed good
chances to score. And after the other games,
Frumkin had complimented him on his play. Today,
nothing. Maybe he was pressing the offense too
much. They had lost control in midfield a lot.

After sitting and stewing for a while, Justin got

bored. He decided to go out and walk around.

"Where you headed?" Cosimo asked.

"Out."

"Want to kick a ball around?"

Justin and Cosimo passed a ball back and forth through the woods and then found an empty field. They took turns juggling the ball, then kicking and trapping.

"Still kicking with a straight leg?" Cosimo asked.

"Am I?"

"I think so."

Justin took the ball and tried kicking it. He *was* straightening his knee.

"Yeah, I am. I don't know about that bent-knee stuff anyway. I mean, doesn't it make more sense to have a solid, locked leg? If your knee is bent, then there's more give, you know?"

Cosimo tried it.

"I see what you mean. Still, Ian seemed pretty sure about it."

"Maybe there are different ways to kick with power," Justin said.

Justin tried kicking with the bent leg. He could kick the ball a long way, but he always hit floaters. He tried to keep his toe down, and hit one good drive, but he was getting confused. He knew he was supposed to land on his kicking foot, but he always felt totally off-balance when he tried it that way.

They played for a little while longer, then headed back to the bunk. Justin decided he was just thinking too much about scoring. He would get his goals. Anyway, center midfield was really a playmaking position. Strikers were the scorers. He should be happy to collect assists, and win games.

Especially tomorrow's game. It was against Wisconsin—and Brian Packer.

8

Justin took Dana's pass on the run. Angling away from the player marking him, he broke free. As he dribbled he glanced around. The Vultures had a momentary man advantage, four on three. Cosimo was on the left, even with the defense; he was slowing down to stay onside.

It was the second half of a tight contest with Bunk Wisconsin. The score was one-all.

Justin stopped and passed safely to Kirk, who quickly passed over to Nick. Nick was playing striker for today's game and scored the Vultures' lone goal in the first half on a sweet-curving shot from fifteen yards out.

Nick was tackled, but he turned on his man and took the ball deep on the right side. He set and tried a long cross to Cosimo, who couldn't handle the ball. It bounded out to Kirk, who was free and twenty yards out. Justin circled in from the left. He was wide open and waved his hands for the pass.

Kirk moved in, and as a defender approached, shot. It was a high, looping shot, and the Wisconsin goalkeeper snared it in the air. The Vultures turned upfield in retreat.

"Hey, Kirk, I was wide open!" Justin yelled as they ran together.

"I saw you, but I had a shot."

"I was wide open!"

"Okay, okay, I'm sorry."

Justin had been in perfect position. All it would have taken was a halfway-decent pass and he would have had a point-blank shot.

The momentum turned to Wisconsin. Brian Packer was a one-man team, taking the ball on long run after long run. He was so good he could get away with it. The boys from Vermont just couldn't seem to recapture the ball. Marty made two great saves to keep the score knotted at one. Time was running out.

Brian again had the ball for Wisconsin, but this time Justin came after him and made a good hard sliding tackle. It was tough, but legal. Justin leapt up and got to the loose ball.

He headed upfield, but Brian tore after him and threw a brutal sliding tackle from behind. The counselor who was refereeing blew his whistle immediately. It was an obvious foul, and *this* game, they were being called.

Justin leapt to his feet angrily.

"Cheap-shot artist!" Justin yelled. Brian pushed him away with both hands. Justin jumped at him and the two pounded at each other before the counselor pulled them apart.

Brian was shown the red card—taken out of the game—and Wisconsin had to finish a man down.

"Well, at least the referee threw out the right guy," Nick said. "But I have to call the fight a draw."

"What are you talking about? I got him a dozen good times in the gut."

"Yeah, and took a dozen yourself. What a couple of ham-bone sluggers."

Justin felt his sore cheekbone. "Maybe you're right."

Vermont took the free kick. Without Brian, Wisconsin was vulnerable, but was there enough time?

The Vultures moved downfield, but lost the ball. Possession went back and forth. Finally, Kirk made a great tackle to strip the ball. Justin took it and led a charge. They had a man advantage. Justin passed to Tony. Always fast on his feet, Tony dribbled around the defender, who tripped himself up and fell. Now Vermont was in a perfect spot. The Wisconsin goalie had no choice but to range out to cut off the angle. Tony went to Kirk on the right and he promptly centered the ball to Justin.

The goalie was totally out of position. Justin took the shot. It was unstoppable, but just as it was headed in, Nick caught up to it and nailed it home. Vermont took the lead.

Justin couldn't believe it. He was happy they were up a goal, but he had already chalked up that score—when it was turned into just another assist.

After the celebration, they returned to play, but time quickly ran out and the referee sounded the final whistle. The two teams lined up and shook hands, then came off the field.

"Great game, everyone!" Ian said, clapping his hands as his team walked in. "Kirk! What a cross! A thing of beauty, lad, a true thing of beauty!"

Ian's words made Justin realize how foolish he was being. Why was he so worried about scoring? Kirk's great pass and Tony's ball-handling had made the play happen. Whether it was Nick's goal or his, it was really Tony and Kirk who had given them the chance.

They headed back to the bunk.

"Great game, Justin," Nick said happily.

"Oh, yeah, thanks," Justin responded. "And thanks for stealing my goal."

He was joking, but as soon as he had said the words he realized that it didn't sound like a joke.

"What?"

"I'm just kidding."

"I shouldn't have kicked it, should I?" Nick asked. "You're right, Justin. It was going in anyway."

"No, that's ridiculous. I was just kidding, really."

"I know you've been kind of bugged by not scoring," Nick continued, but Justin just waved away his comment. Tony and Dana joined them.

"That puts us in first place in the division," Dana said.

"Yeah?" Nick asked.

"Missouri beat Nevada this morning, so we're tied with Nevada at 3–1," Tony said.

"So what good does it do to win the division?" Nick

asked. "Don't we have to win the tournament to be camp champions?"

"Yeah, but it's good to be seeded first in the tourney so you can play worse teams," Dana said.

"Wouldn't it be great to play Wisconsin in the championship?" Tony said.

"Man, that would be great," Cosimo agreed.

"Hey, Justin, there they go now, Team Wisconsin and your buddy Brian," Nick said, pointing over to where Brian and some of the other Wisconsin players were walking. "Maybe you should go beat him up."

"No, thanks." Justin grinned. "What a jerk."

"C'mon, you can take him," Dana said. "He's only a foot taller and thirty pounds heavier than you."

"He was really ticked off when I tackled him." Justin added, "You should have seen his face."

"I did." Tony laughed. "The guy almost had a fit."

"Just because Brian's been to this camp before, he thinks he should get special privileges."

"If we play again I'll give him a special-privilege line drive to the gut," Dana said.

"I have a feeling that Brian isn't the type to forgive and forget," Tony said.

"I think you're right," Justin agreed. "Guess I've got an enemy for life."

9

"Two touches, Justin! Get the pass off!" Frumkin called out.

Justin lost the ball, then turned and scrambled back, trying to catch his man.

Vermont was working out on the small practice fields that afternoon. They were playing a three-on-three game with a two-touch limit. Each player was only allowed to touch the ball twice each possession. The idea was to eliminate long runs, teach good passing, play with heads up, and, most of all, to keep the goal as the target.

Kirk took the ball, passed to Lou, who passed immediately to Woody, who went back to Kirk, who shot and scored.

"That's the way!" Frumkin cheered. "Catch them committing to offense."

Justin took the ball. This three-on-three business was tough. One slip set up a scoring opportunity for the other side.

He passed to Cosimo, who went to Steve. Steve deflected the pass behind his marking man and then circled after it.

"Great, Stevie, now cross!"

Steve passed across to Justin, who brought the ball under control and took the shot. It was on goal, but high, going over the crossbar.

"Get over the ball, Justin," Ian corrected. "Got to get your toe down to keep the ball *down*. All right, next group in. Let's go! Remember, two touches, so you've got to be thinking a few steps ahead. You've got to know where your next pass is going *before* you get the ball."

Justin and the others moved off the field as six new players moved on. While off, they were supposed to practice kicking and trapping, but Justin sat down on the grass to catch his breath. He was getting tired of constantly kicking around. Michael scored a header on a pass from Nick.

"Nice play," said Cosimo, who was sitting by Justin.

"Yeah," Justin said.

"Everyone is getting better," Cosimo went on. "The team is really coming together."

"Everyone but me," Justin said.

"What do you mean?"

"I don't know. Nothing."

Justin had started out as one of the best, but now he wondered where he stood. Maybe soccer was like all the other sports he played. He was good, but not great. Ian and Frumkin always seemed to be criticizing his play, and even in this little three-on-three he had trouble putting the ball into the goal.

"Hey, we don't need spectators," Frumkin yelled. "Get up and at 'em over there."

Justin and Cosimo climbed to their feet and started kicking a ball back and forth. After a bit, their turn on field came again. Justin walked on slowly.

"What's the matter, Justin, tired?" Frumkin asked.

"No, sorry," Justin said, breaking from a walk to a jog.

"I didn't say this game would be easy, but it forces you to think and it forces you to be aggressive, to take the shot."

Steve took the ball in and passed to Justin, who hit a penetrating pass to Cosimo.

"Now that's a pass, Justin!"

Cosimo shot, drilling the ball powerfully past Marty for the goal.

"Good shot," Justin said. "How do you hit it so hard, Cosmo?"

"I don't know. I just think about where I'm trying to shoot."

Later, Justin got a free shot and hit a curving ball that found the net. A goal at last, but it wasn't satisfying. On the small field, scoring chances came easily, and Justin still hadn't gotten any crunch into the ball.

It was a long hot afternoon, and Frumkin really worked them. After the three-on-three game, they ran more dribbling and heading drills. By the end, everyone was bushed.

They rested up in the bunk for a while, before Nick got most of the guys to come along for a pickup baseball game.

Justin wasn't sure if he wanted to go.

"All right, anyone else? Last call for baseball,"

Nick said. Justin stayed flopped on his bed.

Nick and the others headed out, so only Justin and Kirk were left in the bunk. Justin flipped through an old "Firestorm" comic book he had already read three times.

"Want to go have a kick?" Kirk asked after a while.

"Nah," Justin said. "I'm reading."

"A little practice never hurt anyone."

"I get enough practice already," Justin said. "I'm just glad we've got games every day."

"Well, you'd better not be burned out." Kirk laughed. "We've got two weeks to go."

"True," said Justin.

But he didn't laugh.

10

Weekends at the All-Star camp were days off from the regular schedule. On Saturdays the whole camp piled into buses and went for day-trips. This Saturday they went to an amusement park. Justin spent most of his time sloshing down the water slide and also played three rounds on the miniature golf course. It was fun, and a good break from soccer.

Sundays they got to sleep late and then had open activities in the afternoon. Since it was pouring rain this Sunday, outdoor play was off. A movie was shown in the main lodge and a bingo game was held in the cafeteria. Nick, along with most of the guys in Bunk Vermont, went for bingo, but Justin watched the movie—*20,000 Leagues Under the Sea*—even though he'd seen it before. Afterward, films of old World Cup games were shown. Watching the best players ever—Pelé, Eusabio, Maradona—got Justin psyched up again. It reminded him what a great game soccer was.

Rain was still coming down Monday morning when Ian came into the bunk.

"Sorry, lads, morning practice is off," he announced.

"Just 'cause of the rain?" Dana asked.

"Right-o."

"What about the game against Indiana today?" Nick asked.

"If it doesn't clear up, we'll play two games tomorrow."

The rain did stop and the sun was shining when the lunch call blew. Still, afternoon games were canceled, to give the fields time to dry out.

It was a good thing practice was scheduled in the gym that afternoon. All the guys were getting cabin fever. They played a game of seven-on-seven, with Frumkin and Ian playing, but with so little room to maneuver, Justin felt like he was inside a pinball machine. He scored a goal on a pass from Nick. Afterward, they hit the shower house.

"I hope it doesn't rain anymore," Justin said, lathering his hair. "It seems like we haven't played real soccer in a week."

"I liked playing in the gym," Nick said. "It was crazy, with the ball bouncing around so wildly."

"I figured you liked it, too, Justin," said Dana. "Mr. Assist finally got a goal."

"What's that supposed to mean?" Justin snapped.

"You got to score, for once," Dana snapped right back.

Justin was angry. "How many goals have you scored, Edwards?"

"Defensemen aren't supposed to score—anyway, I did get one, too."

"Well, for your information, center midfielders aren't goal scorers either. Ever hear of a playmaker?"

"Yeah, a playmaker who's missed every chance he had," Kirk joined in.

"Cram it, Flaherty," Justin barked. "The only reason you ever score is 'cause you go and hang by the net."

"You think you're so hot," Kirk teased, "just because you can do your little juggling tricks, Captain Justin."

"Yeah, Captain," Dana laughed.

Justin clammed up.

"What's the matter, Justin, can't take a joke?" Kirk said.

"Hey, maybe we can ask Frumkin to trade Justin to another team?" Dana suggested jokingly. "Why don't we trade him for Brian Packer?"

Everyone but Justin laughed.

"Yeah," Kirk agreed. "Brian's a jerk, but he does score goals."

As Justin stayed silent, the teasing stopped. He wasn't going to forget the insults. All his doubts returned. No one would think he was any good until he started scoring goals. He'd do it, then. One way or another.

Tuesday morning was sunny and hot, and the fields were ready. Games began right after breakfast, starting off with all the make-up games.

As the Vultures took the field, Dana walked up to Justin.

"Gonna score today, Justin?"

"Ha, ha," Justin said sarcastically.

"We were just kidding," Dana said.

"Oh sure, sure, it was a laugh riot," Justin said.

"Just forget it. You play defense, I'll get assists."

"All right."

But Justin didn't mean it. He was going to score a goal if it killed him.

Indiana controlled the game early. They had a solid midfield that worked the ball with short passes. Only two great saves by Marty kept Vermont in it. At halftime it was still a scoreless game.

In the second half, Vermont made a break on a great clearing pass from Steve up the left sideline to Cosimo. Justin could smell a scoring chance as he sprinted upfield. Cosimo centered to him, and he dropped it back to Kirk. Justin ran straight down as Kirk passed to Woody on the run. Woody made a swell move to beat his man and then saw Justin in the clear. Justin was running with a hand up, signaling, hoping desperately that Woody could get the ball to him.

Woody was stopped by a defender, and passed across. It was a beauty. Justin ran and trapped the ball on the outside of his foot, with no one between him and the keeper. Two more steps and a shot would do it, but the whistle pierced his concentration.

"Offside!"

Justin glanced around quickly and slapped his head. He *was* yards offside. It wasn't even close.

That was as near as Justin came to a goal that game. Cosimo scored on a corner kick from Woody and the defense held, giving the Vultures their fifth victory against one loss.

Justin tried to be happy, for the team.

11

After playing Indiana in the morning, the Vultures quickly grew tired as they took on the boys from Iowa. Frumkin had made some shifts for the game. He wanted to give players experience in different areas. Justin was still at center half, but Michael and Steve came up to play strikers while Cosimo and Kirk went back to defense. Fortunately, Iowa had also played that morning, and they weren't that good a team. Their record was 2–3 so far.

Woody Widmer scored the first goal of the game

on a long shot that found the upper corner of the net.

"Wow! What a shot," Michael said, as the front lines surrounded Woody.

"Twenty yards easy!" Nick exclaimed.

As they jogged back upfield, Nick and Justin were still shaking their heads in amazement.

"What was he even thinking, taking a shot from there?" Justin said.

"Hey, he must have known something," Nick laughed.

"For a goofy-looking guy, he sure can play."

"You said it."

In the second half, Iowa scored on a penalty shot after Cosimo tripped one of the opposing strikers. The game stayed tied until midway through the period, when Vermont had a corner kick. Woody lined it up, as Justin scrambled to get the offense into position.

Woody floated the ball high to the near side of the goal. Justin had his eye on it the whole way. He was being closely marked, but he circled tightly around another Iowa player and squirted free. An Iowa defenseman leapt high, trying to head the ball away, but mistimed his jump. The ball came down. The goalie was coming after it. Justin dove and got there first, heading the ball solidly into the back of the net. Goal!

As Justin got up he saw Woody run in and do a somersault. In a moment Justin was surrounded by happy teammates, slapping his back.

"Terrific dive!" Kirk said.

"Yeah! You really used your head!" Nick agreed. They all groaned.

"You should have seen yourself," said Woody. "I wish I had the highlight film of that one. You were laid flat-out in the air. Woo!"

As they calmed themselves to resume play, Nick and Justin ran together.

"Well, there it is at last, pal," Nick said. "Goal number one."

"Doesn't count," Justin said.

"Doesn't count!?"

"Doesn't prove I can kick, does it?"

"You're impossible."

"Hey, I'm happy."

"You'd better be."

"But it doesn't count."

Vermont held the lead as both sides grew exhausted. When it was over, a 2–1 victory, they collapsed on the sideline.

"Great game, lads," Ian said. "Now we head to the

practice field for some three-on-two drills."

"What!" called the half-dozen voices.

"Just kidding, just kidding. Boy, you Americans have no sense of humor."

As the rest of the players headed back to the bunk, Justin stayed behind. He wanted to talk to Ian, who was watching the next game get under way.

"Ian?"

"Justin Johnson."

"Can I get some advice?"

"That's what I flew four thousand miles for."

"I've got to get a goal-scoring kick."

"Oh, well, I've got one right here. . . . What do you mean?"

"I don't have enough power. I've got to score goals."

Ian got serious.

"You've played very well, Justin. You're the maestro, the playmaker. Goals aren't everything."

"C'mon."

"You're the best center half I've seen here at camp. Don't worry about goals. They'll come."

"But I've had my chances. I just never have enough, well, oomph, you know."

"All right, get your ball and come along."

Ian and Justin walked to the practice field. Along

one side some big wooden backboards were set up. They stopped in front of one.

"It is true, Justin, your scoring drives aren't powerful," Ian began. "And it's for the same reasons I've told you before. You've got your knee bent now, but your weight transfer and the position of your toe are still making you loft the ball."

"Isn't there anything else?"

"There's no magic trick to it, lad."

Justin wished there were. Ian had him kick against the board for a while, but Justin just couldn't get the hang of keeping his weight over the ball. He felt like he was falling down. Still, Ian thought he was improving.

"That's it, listen to that ball pound."

"I don't know, Ian. Maybe I'm just not strong enough."

"Don't be dull. It's technique that does the job. The ball only weighs fifteen ounces."

They hit for a few more minutes. After Ian left, Justin stayed a while longer, battering the ball as hard as he could.

When he arrived back at the bunk, Justin couldn't believe what he saw. The bunk was in a shambles. Everything was knocked off the shelves. The bedsheets and blankets were pulled from all the beds.

It was a disaster area. The guys were slowly putting things back in order.

"What happened?" Justin asked.

"Bunk raid," Marty moaned, collecting comic books from off the floor.

"Who did it?"

"It was like this when we got back," Nick said.

"I've got a pretty good idea who it was, though," Tony said. "Wisconsin."

"Led by none other than Brian 'The Rat' Packer," Nick sneered.

"Is that guy still after you, Tony?" Justin asked, beginning to sort through his spilled things.

"Constantly. Everywhere I go, Packer is there with a water balloon. He steps on the heels of my sneakers. He's a constant pain."

"Well, you did mash his hand into his dessert," Marty laughed.

"Only because he stole mine."

"We're gonna raid them back," Woody said.

"Oh, no, you're not," Frumkin said from the corner. Justin noticed that the counselors' beds and shelves had been left alone.

"I've already had a chat with Larry, Wisconsin's counselor," Frumkin said. "And they are being punished."

"Right, how? Getting their knuckles rapped?" Nick asked.

"No, as a matter of fact, don't look for Brian and company at next Saturday's outing."

"Seriously?" Tony asked.

"Wow, that's harsh," Woody said.

"And unless Bunk Vermont would also like to spend that day here in camp on cleanup duty," Frumkin warned, "there will be no counterraid. Got it?"

They all agreed. For now.

12

Justin splashed through the foot-deep water along the shore. He ran all the way to one side, then turned and ran all the way back across. It was tiring, but he could feel his thigh muscles working. He ran two more laps, splashing along, before he noticed that Nick was watching him. He waved hello but kept plowing through the water.

"Swimming would be more fun," Nick said with a straight face. "You only have to go a little deeper."

"I've got to build up my leg muscles," Justin said.

"I get it." Nick nodded. "So you can kick the ball harder, and score goals."

Justin shrugged.

"Did Ian tell you that?"

"No, I read about running in water in some magazine. Ian just gave me the same old advice."

"Did you ever think of taking it?"

"I have! I've worked like crazy to figure out that stupid weight-transfer business. It just doesn't work."

"All right, all right. Forget it."

They did some diving off the board and then swam in. They were going to play Oklahoma that afternoon.

When it was time for the game, it got off to a fast pace. The Vultures scored first when a desperate defender tripped Cosimo in the penalty area. Cosimo converted the penalty kick with a hard low shot. The Oklahoma goaltender had no chance, but his teammates quickly evened the score with a follow-up to a long shot that Marty saved, but couldn't hold.

Oklahoma controlled the tempo. Justin was beginning to regret his morning exercise. He was bushed even before the end of the half. He tried to conserve his energy, but he was always a few steps behind his opponents.

Over the short halftime break Justin felt refreshed, but as soon as he hit the field again he knew he was kidding himself. His legs were beat. They ached. But he knew he had to give his all and hope it was enough.

On a long clearing pass from Dana, quickly recaptured by Oklahoma, Justin's man made a run upfield. Justin gave chase. The guy stopped the ball, then faked left and right as Justin jumped back and forth. Finally, he went sideline, burning Justin, who didn't have anything left. Luckily, Kirk was there and forced the ball out of bounds.

As the ball was retrieved and Vermont readied themselves for the throw-in, Justin stooped over trying to catch his breath.

"You all right?" Kirk asked.

Justin tried to nod convincingly. He couldn't speak.

"You look pretty wiped."

"I'm all right," Justin finally managed. "Don't worry about me."

Ian must have noticed, because he substituted for Justin at the next stoppage of play. He didn't say anything, though. While Justin watched from the side, the two teams again traded goals to make it 2–2. After ten minutes, Ian sent Justin back in.

Nick threw the ball and Woody brought it up the right side. A pass to Cosimo was poorly placed, making it a fifty-fifty ball for him and the defender. They arrived at the same time, with Cosimo sliding to tackle the ball. Neither controlled as the ball glanced free. Justin ran toward it, but an Oklahoma player beat him to it, sending a long clearing pass across the field.

Justin turned to sprint back, knowing that too many Vermont players had committed themselves upfield, but as he turned he felt a twinge and then the pull. His right thigh suddenly contracted in the most painful cramp Justin had ever had. It felt like a knife in his leg. He tried to take another step, but it hurt too much. He collapsed on the ground, clutching his leg.

Ian was there in an instant.

"Where is it?"

"Thigh."

"You've got to straighten out the leg," Ian said, grabbing Justin's leg and roughly massaging the muscle. As Ian worked, Justin felt the sharp pain subside to an ache. He looked downfield.

"They're still playing!" Justin exclaimed.

"Can't stop a breakaway for an injury."

Justin watched as the ball went into a crowd in

front of the net. Suddenly, out it came, a shot that Marty dove after helplessly. Oklahoma took a 3–2 lead. The Vultures' players gathered around Justin.

"You all right?" Nick asked.

"What is it?" Cosimo asked.

"He's okay, lads, just a bad cramp," Ian answered. "All right, Justin, now try to walk it off—but don't flex your knee up. You don't want to let that muscle get tight again."

Justin felt stupid limping off the field. A lousy cramp, and it had cost them a goal, and maybe the game! He was certain that if he had been able to get back he could have helped out.

Watching the final minutes of the game from the sideline, with his legs stretched out, Justin was angry at himself. He knew it was dumb to think he could build up his muscles in one day. His desperation to become a goal scorer was making him act foolish.

The game ended without another goal; Oklahoma won 3–2. Vermont's record fell to five wins and two losses. Justin blamed himself.

13

"If you've got to score goals, Justin," Frumkin said, "then you should be playing the attack, not center middie."

"But center half can be an offensive position," Justin protested, as they walked back from breakfast.

"You can go to goal from anywhere, but you seem to be concerned with racking up high totals."

"I just want to prove that I can score," Justin said.

"You're also afraid that if you don't score goals, your pals won't remember how good you are."

"No. I don't know. Maybe."

"Look," Frumkin suggested, "we'll put you up front and see how it goes. You'll get your chances. Maybe the midfield will collapse, maybe it won't. Anyway, you're here to learn the game and you should get experience at a variety of positions, right?"

"I guess so."

"But remember this, Justin. Score or no, you're a fine player. You're what makes Vermont go."

Justin glowed at the compliment. He hadn't felt so good since the second day of camp.

When Vermont took the field to play Missouri, Justin was in an unfamiliar spot: the front line. Cosimo took over at center half. Justin reminded himself not to roam too far back on defense, and not to charge offside on the other end.

The first half of the game offered nothing but frustration. Missouri dominated the play with short, accurate passing, so that Justin hardly got out of breath. At the same time, Cosimo was having a lot of trouble adjusting to his new role. He was holding the ball too long, trying to set up penetrating passes when he should have just kept on the move. Missouri scored twice in the first half.

After the half, Ian and Frumkin put Kirk in at center midfield, but it didn't make much difference. They were still having trouble linking passes.

Then Woody took a pass from Dana and made a long run from his right midfield spot. Kirk, Steve, and Justin spread themselves as they ran with him. Woody stopped and turned on his defender thirty yards out and well to the right. He hit a risky long pass in Steve's direction that bounced free. Kirk picked it up and shot, but a Missouri defender jumped in the way. The ball bounced hard back toward the right where Woody took a shot. It was a good one. The Missouri goalie dove but could only deflect it. A defenseman was on the ball, but Justin came at him from his blind side, kicking the ball right out from under him and into the back of the net. Justin had scored at last.

As he was mobbed by teammates, Justin was pleased, but there was still a nagging feeling bothering him.

Michael approached Justin.

"I'm substituting in for you," he said.

"All right, go get 'em," Justin said, as they slapped hands.

On the sidelines, Justin found that Nick was also out.

"Nice goal, Justin."

"Yeah."

"Don't tell me there's something wrong with this one, too?" Nick laughed. "It was a legitimate, kicked goal. Chalk it up in the record book."

"Yeah, but switching positions was a cheap way to get one."

"What do you mean?"

"I shouldn't have asked Frumkin to move me up to striker. Anybody on this team would have scored that goal. It doesn't prove anything."

"One thing's for sure," Nick said, "we sure miss your ball-handling in midfield."

"I agree," Frumkin interjected. Justin was embarrassed that they'd been overheard. Frumkin continued: "Back to center half?"

"Okay," Justin said.

At the next throw-in, Justin went in for Kirk while Nick took over for Lou at stopper. Vermont still trailed 2–1. Playing with newfound enthusiasm, Justin led the comeback. Twice, great scoring chances were thwarted only by great saves by the Missouri net-minder. Time was running out.

The next break for Vermont found Justin with the ball twenty yards out. He made a run straight at the defense. Two Missouri players quickly converged on him. At once, he stepped over the ball, using his heel to make a deft back pass to Dana, who was following the play. In the clear, Dana hit a shot like a cannon. Untouched, the ball found the upper left net and the game was tied at two-all.

Within a minute after the score, the final whistle blew and it was over. There were no overtimes in the regular games. Tie or no, Vermont was happy with their comeback.

As Justin, Nick, Tony, and Woody walked across camp back to the bunk, they crossed paths with some of the guys from Bunk Nevada.

"Who'd you guys play?" one of them asked.

"Missouri," Tony said.

"How'd you do?"

"We won," Nick said, "two to two." The boys from Vermont laughed, while the others looked at them strangely and kept on their way.

Friday, Justin was back at his familiar center mid-field position for the start of the Michigan game. It was the last game of the camp's regular season. After the weekend, the final tournament would begin. Going into this final game, the Vultures' record was 5–2–1.

As soon as play got underway, Justin realized that center half was where he wanted to be, where he belonged. There was never a free moment. He was always running, always moving, always involved.

Justin led a run beginning with a give-and-go to Cosimo. Justin beat one man on the dribble and then crossed back to Kirk who hit a line drive on goal. A Michigan defenseman made a fantastic header to clear the ball wide of the net. Woody's corner kick was snatched high in the air by the goalie.

"Tough break, Kirk," Justin panted as they returned downfield. "Thought you had it."

"They made a great play on it, didn't they?" Kirk said shaking his head. "The way everyone is improving, it's getting tougher to score around here."

As play continued, Justin realized that Kirk was right. Since the early days of camp the level of play had really improved. That was the whole point of camp, of course, but Justin hadn't really noticed it until now. He had been so worried about his own problems.

On his next possession, Justin was tackled hard, and lost the ball. Luckily, Kirk beat the Michigan man to the fifty-fifty ball, and found Woody with a back pass. Justin was again impressed by the skill of the opposition. When he had first arrived, it seemed he could control the ball for as long as he pleased. Now he was having to play team soccer.

The game went well into the second half without a score. Justin was getting frustrated. He had one great opportunity to go to goal, but tried to put too much power behind it and ended up squibbing it as he lost his balance. Climbing up from the ground, Justin found he had lost all the enthusiasm that had come with switching back to center half. He hadn't solved his problem. He still couldn't score a goal to save his life, and what's more, with everyone improving so much, he was feeling more and more like an average player.

Finally, Vermont pushed the ball deep and caused a traffic jam ten yards in front of the Michigan net. Somehow, Woody got a free leg into the crowd and stung the ball along the ground to score the game's first and only goal. Ten minutes later, it was over. The Vultures celebrated the end of their 6–2–1 season, but Justin coudn't muster much enthusiasm.

"Play-offs here we come!" Woody yelped.

"*Championship* here we come!" Nick corrected loudly.

Lake, here I come, Justin thought to himself. He was sore and tired. A little swim would be just the thing. He wasn't in the mood to share his teammates' rowdiness.

14

After breakfast Saturday, the whole camp was buzzing with excitement as the buses pulled in for the second big outing. The counselors were keeping their destination a secret, but veteran campers said that they always went to a county fair, then to a park that had a great swimming creek.

Justin, Nick, Kirk, and Tony had been ready to go since before breakfast, so when the bus doors swung open, they climbed aboard. They nabbed seats in the back of the bus.

"This is going to be great!" Nick exclaimed.

"You don't even know where we're going," Justin said.

"Yes, but wherever it is, there's got to be a Dairy Queen somewhere along the way."

"Yeah, but who says we'll stop there?" Tony asked.

"If we don't, I'm just going to leap for it," Nick said, and the others laughed.

The bus filled quickly and soon the driver got behind the wheel while counselors took a head count.

"Hey, look, you guys," Kirk said. "There's Bunk Wisconsin."

Through the open bus windows, they could see an unhappy group of campers sitting on a fence watching the buses.

"Wow," Tony said. "Frumkin wasn't kidding. They really aren't going."

Kirk stuck his head out the window and yelled at the Wisconsin team: "Hey, what's the matter with you guys? Don't you want to come?"

They ignored him. Now the rest of the bus was looking on, too. Tony took over the window. "Hey, Brian! Brian Packer!"

When Brian looked, Tony turned, tugged down his shorts, and shined a moon out the window just as the bus began to move. Howls of laughter filled the bus.

Outside, Brian was hopping mad. He yelled and pointed: "Tony Fripp—you're a dead man!"

"Scared, Tony?" Kirk asked.

"Petrified!" Tony said, pretending to shake. Then he added seriously: "Brian doesn't scare me. I can take him."

"Take him in a fight?" Justin asked, disbelievingly.

"He's got three inches and forty pounds on you," Kirk pointed out.

"The bigger they come . . ." Tony began.

"The harder they hit," Nick interjected, and they all laughed.

Justin was amazed at Tony's confidence. Brian wasn't flabby, he was strong, and big. But Tony really seemed to think he could take him on.

The day was great. Away from the soccer field, Justin found he could relax and have a good time. As predicted, the county fair was their first stop, complete with rides, games, and some wild exhibits. Then they hit the park for a great cookout lunch and in the afternoon they went inner-tube rafting on the creek. It was a blast. On the way home they stampeded a McDonald's for dinner and stopped at

Dairy Queen, too. When they finally rolled into camp, it was dark. Justin had no trouble getting to sleep.

Sunday morning at camp was slow and easy. Most of Bunk Vermont was still asleep when Nick and Justin tiptoed out and headed for the mess hall.

Nick poured himself a big bowl of Captain Crunch. Justin reached for the Grape-Nuts.

"Augh!" Nick said. "How can you eat that road gravel?"

"It's good."

"No, it's not," Nick corrected. "It's good *for* you."

"Guess I'm weird."

"You know what your problem is?" Nick said. "You're not really a kid at all, you're an undersized grown-up."

"The ultimate insult." Justin laughed.

"You know, it's kind of true," Nick said seriously. "Here's an example. You're smart, right? A brain? You even think you're smarter than Ian or Frumkin."

"No, I don't."

"Well, you think you can figure out how to kick for power better than they can."

"That's not true. I listen to their advice."

"Yeah, you listen, ignore it, then go run around

in two feet of water until your legs cramp up."

"Ha, ha."

"I'm serious," Nick said.

"You're never serious," Justin snapped. Nick's badgering was a pain. "That's your problem. Always goofing off, cracking jokes. You don't pay attention to those guys either."

"I may joke around, but at least I'm trying to improve. And I do listen to Frumkin and Ian. I came here to learn, not to show off."

"What's that supposed to mean?"

"Means you came here so everyone could ooh and ahh about your being able to juggle the ball for nineteen hours."

Justin was going to reply, but Tony arrived and sat down.

"What's going on?" Tony asked, suspecting something was up.

"Nothing," Justin said. Woody and Dana joined them. Justin stewed silently while the others talked. *So now Nick, my one supposed friend, has turned on me,* Justin thought. *He's probably been criticizing me behind my back the whole time.* He wondered if he should have kept his desire to score goals to himself.

But in a moment, Justin's thoughts were interrupted. Wally Phillipson, a camper from Bunk Wisconsin, came to the table.

"Tony. Hey, Fripp."

"Yeah?" Tony said, looking up.

"Brian Packer challenges you to a fight, so if you're not chicken, meet him on the practice field at ten o'clock sharp."

His message delivered, Wally turned and left.

"You gonna go?" Woody asked.

"Sure," Tony said.

"Oh, no," Nick gasped. "I'll run and get the nurse. Woody, you call an ambulance."

"Yup," Tony said. "Brian may need one."

"You're crazy, Tony, Brian's *big!*" Justin exclaimed. "I was lucky he didn't get a chance to kill me when we fought."

"Justin's right," Woody agreed. "You don't have to prove anything. Forget him. If you fight, he'll smear you into the ground like cream cheese."

"I'm going," Tony said with determination. He grabbed half a bagel to munch as he left the table.

Justin and Nick exchanged glances. This could be ugly, but they sure didn't want to miss it. They shoveled the last of their cereal into their mouths and followed. Everyone else came, too.

At ten, Tony and his bunkmates arrived at the

field, where Brian and his friends were waiting. There was no sign of counselors.

Brian stepped forward. Tony took off his watch and handed it to Woody.

The two circled for a moment. Brian balled his hands into fists. Tony stayed low, in wrestling form. Both sides yelled encouragement.

"No mercy, Brian!"

"Bust him, Tony!"

Brian attacked, swinging but missing. In a flash, Tony had him by both legs. Justin watched in disbelief as Tony lifted Brian into the air, ignoring Brian's pummeling of his back, twisted him, and then drove him headfirst into the ground. The bigger boy tried to get up, but Tony threw a leg sweep, collapsing him again.

"He's whaling on him!" Nick called out happily.

"Crush him!" Justin yelled.

Tony was riding Brian in a tight half nelson, pulling away Brian's free arm every time he tried to get up.

"Had enough?" Tony barked.

"Cram it!" Brian yelled, so Tony twisted his arm harder. Then Tony let him up, pushing him away.

Brian glared at his smaller opponent, a smear of dirt and grass across his cheek.

He came after Tony again, swinging and flailing. Missing his punches, he kicked at him in frustration. Tony grabbed his foot.

"Kicking's a no-no, Brian," Tony chided. Then with a twist of the leg, he pulled himself closer and pulled away Brian's other leg, again driving him to the ground. Before Brian could move, Tony was on him again, with a headlock.

Brian squirmed.

"I give!" he said, finally.

"Say uncle."

"Uncle."

"Say itty-bitty pretty please."

Brian squirmed again, but Tony tightened his hold until Brian repeated: "Itty-bitty pretty please."

Tony stepped off him. Brian rolled to a sitting position, spitting dirt and grass out of his mouth. Tony was quickly surrounded by his supporters.

"Wicked!" Woody yelled.

"What moves! What style," Nick laughed. "A massacre!"

Tony shrugged.

"You don't have to be big," he said. "If you know what you're doing."

Justin walked behind the crowd as they returned to the bunk. He knew Tony was right. Nick was right. Ian was right. Technique was what Justin needed. He had been bullheaded about doing things his own way. He had to start listening to what the coaches were teaching. Camp was never meant to be three weeks in the spotlight—it was a chance to *learn*.

Justin had to learn a better shot. Once he did that, scoring goals would be as easy as taking on Brian Packer.

15

"We've been through this before," Ian said. He had been reluctant to come out for some early practice, but Justin had begged and pleaded.

"I really appreciate it, Ian," Justin said. "Just give me one more chance. I've got to change. I've got to figure this thing out."

So camper and coach walked out onto the empty field Monday morning and settled in front of one of the backboards. Justin dropped the ball and trapped it.

"We'll go right back to square one, then," Ian said. "What do you kick the ball with?"

Justin didn't get it.

"Your foot."

"Wrong, lad! You kick with your whole body. Your foot strikes the ball. Show me where your foot meets the ball."

Ian continued to tear down Justin's kick until there was nothing left. Then, piece by piece, he put it together again. He had Justin kick using only his follow-through. He had him kick with no follow-through. He had him perform in slow motion. He had him alternate left-footed and right-footed kicks.

Justin grew quickly discouraged, but he was determined to put aside his pride and let Ian teach him.

Finally, Ian let him try the full-motion kick, but only at three-quarters speed. Justin felt awkward, but as he repeated the exercise over and over, it began to feel more natural. He was very aware of keeping his weight shifted until the last possible moment of the kick.

"Okay, my lad," Ian said. "Let's see what kind of pace you can put on the ball now."

Justin kicked, his weight forward over the ball,

his knee bent. The ball flew inches above the ground. *Thump!* The ball walloped off the backboard and rebounded straight back. Justin trapped it, gave it a roll forward, and hit it again. *Thump!*

"That's it!" Ian roared with approval. "Do you feel it, Justin? Do you feel that spring in your leg?"

Sweating, out of breath, Justin nodded. He did feel it! It was a whole new way to kick the ball.

"Don't stop!" Ian yelled. "Hit it and hit it until you never forget the way it feels."

Justin drove the ball again.

"Careful, don't start pulling your shoulder back on me now."

Again and again, Justin kicked the ball under Ian's careful scrutiny. As other bunks gathered on the field for the regular practice, Ian tousled Justin's hair and they walked off the field.

"Good work, Justin."

"I really appreciate your taking the extra time with me, Ian."

"I never mind coaching when I know someone's paying attention."

Justin returned to the bunk. Vermont was free all morning and then had afternoon practice.

The bunk was empty except for Kirk, who was

reading a comic. They exchanged greetings. Justin flopped onto his bed for a rest. Moments later he took his soccer ball off his shelf and dropped it to the floor. First, he went through his newly learned kick in slow motion. Then he began kicking the ball against the back wall of the bunk.

"That looks *real* exciting," Kirk drawled.

"Sorry, is the noise bothering you?"

"No, it's all right."

Justin kept on kicking the ball. After a minute, Kirk spoke up again: "All right, I give up. What's the point?"

"Nothing, I'm just practicing."

"We have practice every day, games almost every day. There are pickup games going constantly. And that's still not enough for you?"

Justin ignored his question, kicking the ball and retrieving it again.

"Know how many goals I've scored, Kirk?" Justin asked.

"Just in regular games?"

"Yeah."

"I remember that header."

"Well, you remember them all then. One goal."

"That's 'cause you're a midfielder," Kirk said.

"So's Brian Packer and he leads the whole camp in scoring," Justin replied. "I haven't scored because I've been shooting like a dweeb. But you know what?"

"What?"

"I've got a new secret weapon."

16

The Vultures practiced hard on Tuesday. They wanted to start the tournament with a full head of steam. And no one worked harder than Justin. When they took the field Wednesday against Oklahoma, they were ready to avenge their earlier 3–2 loss.

Early in the game, Justin ranged deep into the Vultures' defensive zone to help trap the ball-handler in a double team. Dana tackled the ball and succeeded in getting it to Justin. Turning upfield, Justin saw Cosimo on a fast-break sprint, looking back. He set and sledgehammered the long pass. The ball cleared the defender, but it also cleared Cosimo by a long shot. Before anyone could catch up to it, the ball curved out of bounds. Oklahoma took the throw-in.

"Take it easy, Thunderfoot," Dana laughed. Justin couldn't help smiling.

"It may not have worked," he said as he began to run upfield, "but it sure felt good."

Justin missed his first shot on goal, but it was a tough chance. He barely beat the defense to the ball and, in an attempt to get the shot off quickly, could only loft it. The ball went well over the crossbar. Justin soon got another chance.

It was the shot he'd been dreaming of since he got to camp—a slam dunk, soccer-style.

Woody took a Vermont corner kick, driving the ball across the front of the net head-high. A fullback tried to clear with a header, but he didn't get it far enough. Justin was on it in twelve yards and in one smooth motion, he turned his extra lesson into pay dirt. He blasted the ball home, a low bullet. The goalie sprawled after it too late and Vermont took the 1–0 lead.

"Ka-boom!" Cosimo exclaimed. "What a shot!"

"Justin, baby! A forty-megaton blast," Nick chortled happily.

Basking in the slaps and congratulations of his friends, Justin smiled. *That one counts,* he thought.

Cosimo scored the game's second goal on an assist from Kirk. The game was turning into a rout, as Vermont dominated midfield, seldom allowing Oklahoma to put together three passes in a row.

Justin scored again in the second half. It was another dandy. Kirk had taken a shot from the far right. An Oklahoma fullback stopped the shot and tried to clear it, but his kick bounced crazily off two players just in front of the penalty area. Then it came in Justin's direction.

The ball was coming at him chest-high, but Justin immediately knew he didn't have time to trap it and shoot. The defense was swarming. Instead Justin leapt, turned himself horizontal, and volleyed the ball in midair. Again the goalie sprawled. Again the ball smoked into the back of the net. 4–0, Vermont.

Oklahoma scored a late goal, but couldn't mount a comeback as Vermont continued to play tight ball-control soccer. The final whistle sent Vermont to the semifinals, with a 4–1 victory.

"Not a shabby game, Justin," Ian smiled.

Back in the bunk, Justin got to sit back and get a little glory.

"So he's in midair, like this," Nick said, leaping onto a bed. "Ball comes flying across."

"We were there," Dana laughed.

"Not as close as I was," Nick said. "Justin's floating five feet up."

"Five feet!" Kirk howled.

"Yesss!" Nick declared, holding a hand up to his eye level. "Then: boom! He wheels and fires and there's nothing but a blur. If there'd been no net that ball would still be going!"

Everyone had seen the shots, but they still enjoyed listening to Nick. The tournament was exciting. After lunch and the rest hour, they had a free afternoon. Most of the bunk decided to go watch the game between Wisconsin and Ohio. They would play the winner of that game tomorrow. Besides, they all enjoyed rooting against Brian.

They sat on a shady slope ten yards from the field behind the Ohio bench.

"So Wisconsin's better, right?" Cosimo asked.

"Yeah," Justin said. "They finished five-two-two. Ohio was something like three-four-two. We beat Ohio in the first game of camp."

"Man, that seems like a long time ago," Kirk said.

"Back then we hardly knew each other," Dana mused.

"And now," Nick began in singsong voice, "through patience and understanding, we've learned to totally despise each other."

They all laughed. The game wasn't going well for Ohio, so Vermont had little to cheer about. Wisconsin scored two unanswered goals in the first half and continued to control the game in the second.

"Brian may be a jerk," Tony said, watching Packer dribbling the ball upfield, "but he can sure play this game."

"He's better at soccer than fighting, anyway," Justin cracked.

"We're supposed to be scouting these guys," Dana declared. "What's their weakness? What's our strategy?"

"I think we should have Tony pounce on Brian and . . ." Nick began.

"No, seriously," Justin interrupted. "Dana's right."

"Well, Brian *is* the key to their team," Nick suggested.

"True," Dana nodded. "Should we try to double-team him when we can?"

"Definitely," Justin stated. "If we crowd him constantly, the other guys will have to beat us."

"You know," Dana said, "we've still got to get back at Wisconsin for trashing our bunk."

"Yeah, we've gotta do *something*," Justin agreed.

"I'm going fishing," Nick said suddenly. He walked away.

"Why is he leaving *now?*" Dana asked Justin.

Justin shrugged. "Don't ask me."

They went back to talking strategy. Each Vermont player watched the players that they would be marking. Wisconsin finished with a 3–0 victory. Tomorrow, the semifinals.

17

The Vultures gathered on the sideline.

"Stay loose, now, lads," Ian encouraged. "Don't drink too much of that water, Dana."

Like the others, Justin was still catching his breath. His shirt was soaked through, so he kept walking back and forth to stay loose.

The game was going into sudden-death overtime.

After regulation, they were tied with Wisconsin at 1–1. It had been a battle. They had marked Brian tightly, but he was still able to penetrate their defense. Luckily, Wisconsin really did seem to be a one-man team. Whenever Brian was kept out of play, his teammates played defensively. No one else was an aggressive playmaker—how could they be? All season, Brian had never given them a chance.

Still, Brian was dangerous all by himself. In fact, only a save by Marty on a Wisconsin corner-kick play—with Brian making the shot—had kept the Vultures in the game. Vermont's goal was a great piece of teamwork, as Justin's crossing pass was headed in by Cosimo. However, the bulk of the game had been played in the middle of the field. Scoring chances were few and far between.

If no one scored in either of two ten-minute overtime periods, it would come down to penalty kicks.

After the short break, the two teams took the field again. Play was slow. Everyone was playing carefully, afraid to make a mistake. Justin could see that they had to change strategy if they were going to score.

"C'mon, let's get aggressive," he barked, as Wisconsin controlled. Cosimo was marking the midfielder with the ball. Justin made up his mind to go after it. First he glanced back, catching Dana's eye, to let him know that he was coming off Brian. Waiting until the ball-handler turned away, Justin sprinted over to double-team. The play looked brilliant as Justin and Cosimo moved in, trapping the ball-handler, but then he made a good pass to a fullback, who quickly hit a long, penetrating pass to Brian.

Justin's heart sank. It looked like his play had backfired completely. But it wasn't too late. Dana had seen the play developing and beat Brian to the ball. He hit a left-footed pass to Kirk who stood wide open on the right touchline. Suddenly the advantage was all Vermont. Justin and Cosimo charged downfield, while Woody circled behind Kirk to help out.

Kirk pushed the ball safely to Woody and took off as Woody got the return pass to him perfectly. Kirk dribbled in to force the defense to challenge him, then he hit a low pass toward Cosimo, but another fullback got there at the same time. Cosimo threw a sliding tackle to keep him from clearing. The ball bounded free and Justin gathered it ten yards out. There was never any doubt in his mind. It was go-to-goal time.

The goalie was rushing to cut off the angle. Justin aimed for the near post and let loose. The net-minder sprawled hopelessly after it, but Justin watched in horror as it curved in the air, heading for the post.

It was too far left! But no, the ball hit the post and deflected *into* the goal—Vermont had won!

Justin sprinted back with both fists in the air. He leapt into Dana's arms. The whole team gathered around them.

"What a game! What a goal! What a kick!" Nick yelled.

"We're number one!" Kirk howled.

"Vultures rule!" Dana screamed. He started their victory chant and they all joined in: "Vultures! Vultures! Vultures! Yeahh!!"

When the circle broke up, they calmed themselves long enough to walk through the handshake line, and then howled all the way back to the bunk.

"Man, that's satisfying," Dana said.

"Beating Brian Packer—you said it," Tony agreed. "I don't even care if we win the championship—we beat Brian."

"Thunderfoot rules again," Cosimo said, slapping Nick's shoulder as they entered Bunk Vermont.

"Hey, you made it happen with that stone-hard tackle."

They collapsed on their beds in exhaustion, savoring the victory.

"You know," said Nick, "I hate to mention it, but we still have to win tomorrow."

Eleven pillows flew in his direction. But after they had relived the day's victory for a while, they began to look foward to the championship game. They would be playing the winner of that afternoon's game between Nevada and Missouri.

Justin wondered if even a championship game could ever top the one they had just played.

As it turned out, it couldn't. It wasn't that they weren't psyched up to play the other semifinalist, Nevada. They were. And with the whole camp on the sidelines to watch, every player knew this was a big game. It just didn't have the drama of the Wisconsin game.

Nevada, having beaten Vermont 2–0 earlier in the season, came into the game confident. Their cockiness lasted about two minutes and thirty seconds, when Cosimo hit a long banana shot that curved into the top corner of the net for a score. Justin fed him the pass, to collect an assist.

Five minutes later, Justin took a clearing pass from Dana and put a sweet fake on his man to get by. Charging in on the breakaway, Justin was tripped up from behind. The referee awarded a penalty kick, which Justin easily converted with a cannon shot to the left side. 2–0, Vermont.

The first goal had shocked Nevada; the second one

demoralized them. With 50 minutes yet to play, they seemed to be fading. Taking advantage of their opponents' new uncertainty, Vermont played a tightly controlled short-pass game. Three more good scoring chances were created. Two were saved, the other deflected off the crossbar and over. Meanwhile, back in Vultures' goal, Marty was getting bored. Happily bored.

Nevada regrouped at the half, but it was too little too late. Most of the second half went by scoreless, and when Nevada did finally notch a goal on a corner kick, Vermont came right back. Dana made an end-to-end run and blasted home a twenty-yard coffin nail. The game was as good as over. And then it *was* over. The Vultures were champions, 3–1.

Today's celebration was less wild. They slapped hands and jumped on each other's backs. They tried to pour a bucket of water on Ian and Frumkin, but the counselors were too quick.

At first Justin thought it sounded kind of quiet because yesterday's game had been more dramatic, but he began to realize it was more than that. The championship was their last game together.

Tomorrow, they were going home.

18

Saturday morning was hectic, as all the campers packed up, cleaned up, swapped addresses, and said their good-byes. Tony and Justin took on the task of carrying the bunk's last set of dirty sheets and towels down to the laundry drop. After dumping the load, they headed back.

"Done packing?" Justin asked.

"Not even started," Tony laughed. "You?"

"Actually I'm almost done. I didn't bring much,

and yesterday I traded all my comics to Woody for
his Three Stooges T-shirt."

"Did you have room for the trophy?" Tony asked.
At last night's awards dinner, Justin had won a trophy for being the team's most valuable player, plus
the arm patch that everyone in the bunk got for
winning the championship. Nick had won for "most
improved."

"Yeah." Justin grinned. "I found room for it. I just
threw out all my clothes."

They arrived at Bunk Vermont. With the beds
stripped and most of the shelves empty, Justin was
reminded of the first day of camp, when he didn't
know anyone except Nick. He wondered how many
guys would come back next year. Everyone in Vermont said they wanted to come back, but Dana told
them that everyone in his bunk had said that last
year, too, and only a few had returned.

Justin's father made the three-hour drive from
Cranbrook to pick up his son and Nick, arriving just
after lunch. After a quick tour and a last round of
good-byes, Justin and Nick climbed into the car for
the long ride home.

They told Mr. Johnson all about the season and
the final tournament, about the guys in the bunk,

the coaches, the day-trips. Justin told him how he finally learned a scoring drive. They talked for a while, but the boys had been up late last night and soon the gentle rumbling of the car lulled them to sleep.

When Justin woke up, the scenery along the highway looked familiar and he realized that they were in Cranbrook's outskirts. Nick was already awake.

"We're almost there," he said.

"Seems like we've been gone more than three weeks," Justin said. Nick nodded.

"And we never did get back at Bunk Wisconsin for trashing us," Justin remembered. "Except by beating them."

"Didn't we?" Nick said with a smile, whispering so Mr. Johnson wouldn't hear.

"What'd you do?" Justin whispered.

"Well, you know I went fishing, right?"

"Yeah. So?"

"So, I snuck some little presents in Brian and Wally's trunks."

"What?"

"Oh, just some nice fresh lake fish."

"No. You didn't."

"Yes, I did," Nick said with a wide grin. "By the

time they open their trunks . . ." He held his nose.

They both laughed.

Mr. Johnson exited the highway and drove across Cranbrook. When he took a turn toward their house, Justin said: "Hey, Dad, we have to drop off Nick at his house first."

"Yes, well, I have to pick up something at home before we do."

Justin thought his dad was acting strange, but he didn't say anything. As they approached his house, it didn't take long for Justin—and Nick—to figure out what was going on. By the side of the Johnson house, the grill was smoking and both their families were gathered. Their friends Dennis and Sam were out in front playing Frisbee.

"Hey! Check it out!" Nick exclaimed.

"We thought we'd throw a little welcome-back family barbecue," Mr. Johnson said with a laugh. "Looks like they started without you, though."

The boys stopped long enough to let their moms hug them, but they quickly found their way to Dennis and Sam. The four slapped hands.

"Welcome back," Dennis said.

"So how was it?" Sam asked.

"You are looking at the camp champions!" Nick boasted. "No autographs, no autographs, please."

"It was great," Justin said. "We practiced with really great coaches. One of them was from England. And we had games almost every day."

Nick and Justin kept talking about camp as they tossed the Frisbee around. Then Sam and Dennis filled them in on their Algonquin League baseball season, which was still going on. Soon, Mrs. Johnson called out that the burgers were ready. The boys didn't need to be called twice.

"So, were you the best, Justin?" Sam asked as they walked over. "You're the best soccer player in Cranbrook, so I bet Dennis two bucks you'd be the best player at camp."

"No, there were a lot of good players," Justin said.

"I win," Dennis laughed. "No offense, Justin."

"But Justin was the most valuable player on *the* championship team," Nick said. "That makes him the best player in camp."

"There you go, *I* win," Sam said, poking Dennis in the ribs.

"Well, I was all right," Justin admitted, smiling. "But the best thing is that I'm a lot better than I was before."

"No, that's not the best thing," Nick said, shaking his head.

"Yeah? What is?"

"Only three more weeks until school starts again," Nick said solemnly. Dennis, Sam, and Justin looked at each other.

"Pile on!" Justin yelled and the three of them leapt on Nick before he could get away.

Some comments just *demand* a pile-on.